SCHOOL PICTURE G

PHOTO FIASCOES!

HEY, kids! Which one of these school picture disasters has happened to **YOU**?

Bad hair

Bad skin

Bad everything

Fake smile

DRAW YOURSELF!

Runny nose

Sleepy eyes

Wardrobe failure

You moved!

Also by Lincoln Peirce

Big Nate: In a Class by Himself

Big Nate Strikes Again

Big Nate on a Roll

Big Nate Goes for Broke

Big Nate: In the Zone

Big Nate Lives It Up

Big Nate Blasts Off

Big Nate: What Could Possibly Go Wrong?

Big Nate: Here Goes Nothing

Big Nate: Genius Mode

Big Nate: Mr. Popularity

Lincoln Peirce

BIG NATE
FLIPS OUT

HARPER
An Imprint of HarperCollins*Publishers*

For Nate and Al

www.harpercollinschildrens.com
www.bignatebooks.com
Go to www.bignate.com to read the *Big Nate* comic strip.

ISBN 978-0-06-236752-5

Typography by Sasha Illingworth
18 19 20 PC/LSCH 10 9
❖
First paperback edition, 2016

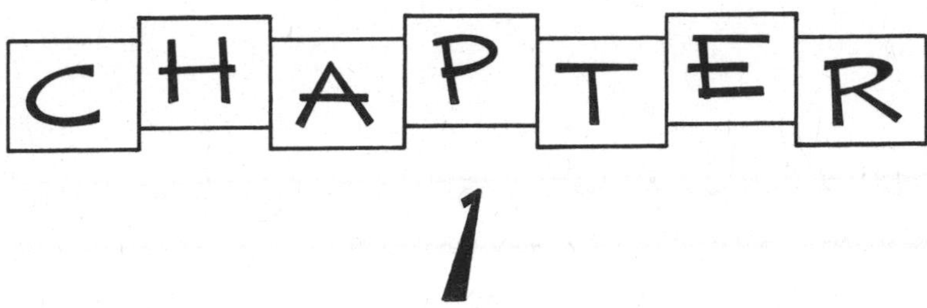

1

"You're such a slob."

I turn around. Francis is shaking his head in disgust.

He rolls his eyes. “No, I was talking to the drinking fountain,” he says. Then he mutters something about “the messiest kid at P.S. 38.”

Just a little background here: P.S. 38 is our middle school. Francis is my best friend. And, yeah, I’m a little messy. So what?

Francis starts to swing his notebook at me, then stops himself. He doesn’t want any teachers to catch him clocking me in the head. Around here, assault with a three-ring binder is worth at least a couple of detentions. And Francis never gets detention. EVER.

See? The detention lady doesn't even know his NAME. That says it all.

People think it's weird that Francis and I are so tight, and do you know what? They've got a point. He and I are total opposites. Here's what I mean:

THE OFFICIAL
"ALL ABOUT FRANCIS"
STUDY GUIDE
1. HE IS A TRIVIA FANATIC
DID YOU KNOW that the pop-up toaster was invented in 1919 by a mechanic named... YAK YAK YAK...
TRIVIA TIME
Hey, I like trivia, too, but it's GOOD trivia, like sports stats and movie lines – stuff you can actually USE.
2. HE'S A STUDYING MACHINE
Francis wants to be an epidemiologist (whatever that is) someday, so he takes school super seriously. But he's not OBNOXIOUS about it.
...like SOME people I know!
Ho hum! Another day, another A! ...PLUS!
A+
Gina
3. HE'S A "CAT PERSON"
Oogie woogie pooky wooky shnooky wiggums!
The less said about this unfortunate part of his personality, the better.

Okay, here's an FYI: Francis isn't really this much of a weenie. I think I wrote this study guide back when I was annoyed with him for hanging air fresheners in our tree house. Anyway, read on.

Maybe the neatness thing should have gone at the TOP of the list. I've known Francis since kindergarten, and he's ALWAYS been Captain Tidypants. Back then, he wouldn't even play in the sandbox without a package of wet wipes.

Oh, brother. "What's the big deal about a crooked poster?" I ask him.

"It looks sloppy," he answers, frowning. "It detracts from the hallway's overall feng shui."

"Hilarious, Teddy," I grumble, rubbing the bump on my head. "You've still got it . . ."

Great. Science with Mr. Galvin. Ever sit through a late-night infomercial for one of those useless kitchen appliances? That's what science is like—except you can't change the channel.

"Nicely done, Gina," Mr. Galvin says. She flashes her usual smirk.

"Francis, great job," he says next. I look over, and Francis holds up his packet so I can see it.

An A! No big surprise there. But it's good news just the same, because Francis and I did the homework together. So if HE got an A . . .

Huh? "See me at my desk"? Where's my "nicely done"? Where's my "great job"?

"Uh . . . okay," I say a little nervously. No, a LOT nervously.

"This is, without a doubt," he announces, his voice rising . . .

I hear snickering behind me. Nice of him to broadcast that little nugget to the entire class. Couldn't he have chewed me out in PRIVATE?

Whatever. I'm not going down without a fight.

"I couldn't even READ your answers!" Mr. Galvin goes on. He's in full-blown rant mode now. "Your HANDWRITING is completely ILLEGIBLE! . . ."

He flips my packet over.

Whoops. Didn't realize I'd started my latest comic masterpiece on the back of my science homework.

"You like mysteries?" he asks, pushing my homework across his desktop.

Yikes, did THIS ever blow up in my face. Three minutes ago I thought I had an A. Now I'm practically getting expelled.

Mr. Galvin's voice follows me as I shuffle back to my seat. "I want that assignment on my desk tomorrow, completely redone."

It's a note from Francis. I sneak a quick peek at Mr. Galvin, who's busy showing Mary Ellen Popowski how to light a Bunsen burner without setting her hair on fire. The coast is clear.

Yeah, I know: You can't read it. You're not SUPPOSED to. Francis and I spend a lot of time making sure that NOBODY can. What good is having a secret code if half the world knows what it means?

Well . . . all right, just so you can follow along, I'll let you see the key. BUT DON'T SHOW IT TO ANYBODY ELSE!

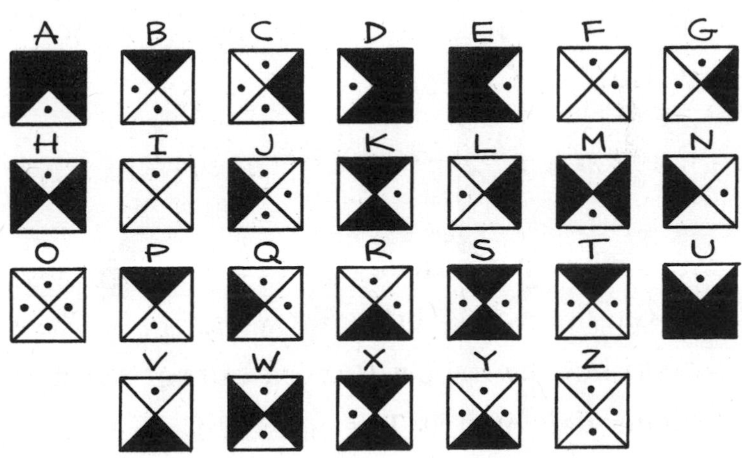

I write back:

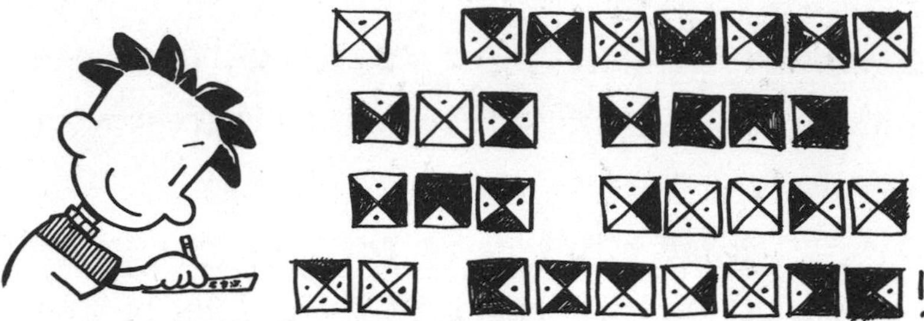

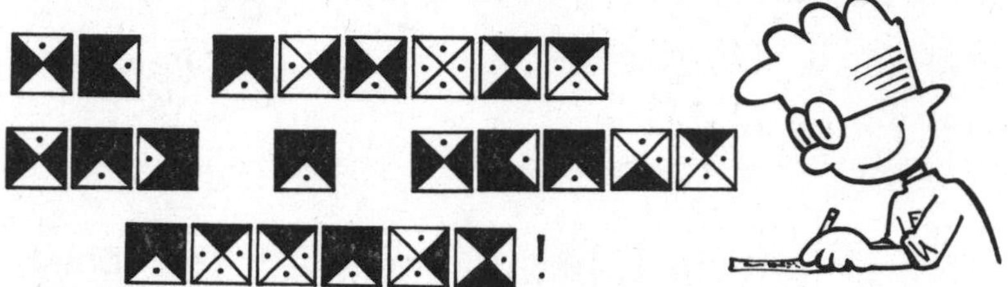

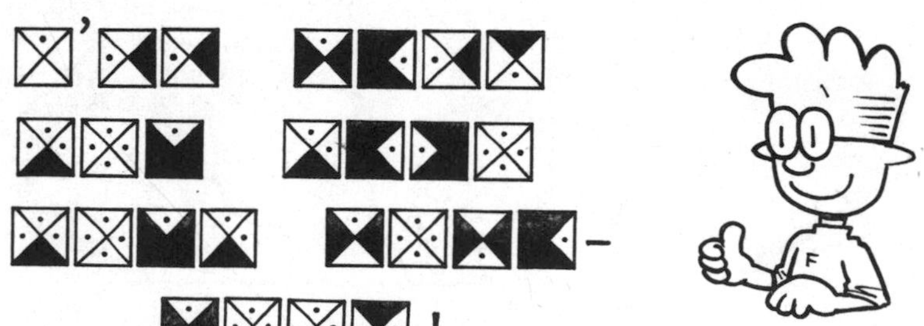

Good ol' Francis.

Finally the bell rings, and we file out. That's the only thing I like about science: It feels great when it's over.

". . . Which is exactly why we should go to the meeting!" Francis says. "Let's make a Chronicle that's MEMORABLE for a change!"

Yeah. For all the wrong reasons.

MAJOR MISTAKES IN LAST YEAR'S "CHRONICLE"

• A bunch of pictures were upside down.

• Next to Chad's name it said: "Most Likely To Be First Woman Elected President."

• The cafetorium ladies were identified as the "Boys Cross-Country Team."

• Practically everybody's name was misspelled. Including...

Frantics Puppy

Tubby Orzits

Nut Weight

What a train wreck. There were more mistakes than Chad has freckles. I started to count them, but I got bored when I hit triple digits.

"You know why all that stuff went wrong, don't you?" Francis asks.

"Sure," Teddy and I answer together . . .

Nick Blonsky was the Chronicle editor last year. I could have told you he'd screw up. Anyone who spends that much time with his finger up his nose doesn't exactly inspire confidence.

"Who's gonna be the editor THIS year?" I ask.

"Well, whoever it is," Francis says as we walk into the meeting . . .

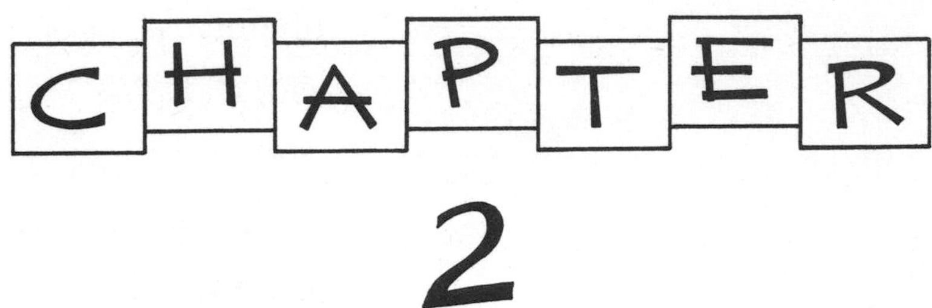
CHAPTER
2

Oh, no. NO!!

NO!

THIS MEETING OF THE YEARBOOK COMMITTEE WILL NOW COME TO **ORDER**!
BAM
BAM
BAM

"GINA?? SHE'S the editor?" Teddy groans.

"Well, what'd you expect?" whispers Francis. "Gina wants to be in charge of EVERYTHING."

Bingo. That's one reason she's about as popular as a fire drill during recess. Here are a few others:

3 Her favorite hobby is getting other people in trouble!
Mr. Galvin, NATE looked at the answers in the back of the textbook after YOU told us NOT to!
URK!
Oh, he DID, did he?
4. Thanks to HER, there's more work for the REST of us!
I finished the worksheet, Mr. Staples!
ALREADY? Guess I didn't make it CHALLENGING enough! I'll fix THAT!
HERE, class! After you complete the FIRST sheet like GINA has, do this ridiculously confusing ADVANCED CALCULUS!
YAY!
What?
Still working on question #1
Chad→

And now back to the meeting, starring Pushy McBossaround.

"OKAY, Gina, we hear you," I tell her. "You can lose the stinkin' hammer."

"It's called a GAVEL, genius . . ."

Nice. Now she's THREATENING us. Is this a yearbook meeting or a game of Whack-A-Mole?

Gina obviously doesn't care that nobody's paying attention to her, because she launches into some bragfest about taking the Chronicle in a "new direction."

"Sounds good," I tell the guys. "She can go HER way . . ."

"Why not?"

Francis nods toward Gina. "Do we really want the yearbook in HER hands?"

Now THAT's bad. You thought a Blonsky-ized Chronicle was scary? A Gina-fied one would be a NIGHTMARE.

"You're right," I say. "We can't just sit here and let Gina make herself the queen of the yearbook."

"So what do we do?" Teddy asks.

"Watch," I whisper. I shoot my hand into the air.

Gina peers at me suspiciously. "What do YOU want?"

Everyone looks stunned. Especially Francis. "ME?" he says.

"ExCUSE me," Gina sputters, her cheeks flushing, "but I'm ALREADY the editor!"

"Oh, is that right? Was there an election? . . ."

Gina's face gets redder. "I VOLUNTEERED, if that's what you mean," she growls. "I volunteered FIRST!"

"And Francis volunteered SECOND," I say. "What's the difference?"

Now she's turning a color I've never even SEEN before. She points the gavel right between my eyes.

"There can't be TWO editors!" she hisses.

That's Mrs. Hickson, the school librarian and yearbook adviser. She's also the only person who's ever sent Gina to detention. And now she's shooting down Little Miss Control Freak's master plan to take over the Chronicle! HA!

I'm really starting to like this woman.

Uh-oh. Maybe I spoke too soon.

She holds up a book. “Recognize this?”

Sure. I just borrowed it from the library last week. “Zack Birdwatcher Takes the Cake.” It was really good. Zack’s this kid who gets a parrot for his birthday, but the parrot disappears. So then . . .

She flips through it. "Perhaps you'd care to explain why there are orange smudges on every single page?"

She frowns. "I see. And what about this STAIN on the cover?"

"And look at THIS!" she goes on.

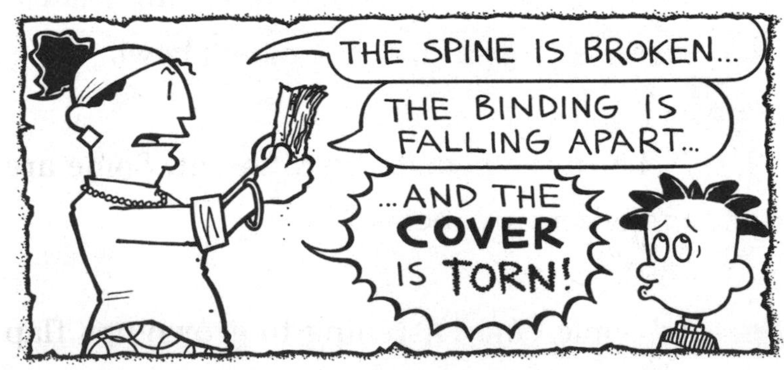

I gulp. It IS pretty beat up. "Uh . . . sometimes stuff gets a little crumpled in my locker."

"A LITTLE CRUMPLED? This looks like it went through a TRASH COMPACTOR," she shouts. Wait, aren't librarians supposed to be QUIET?

Yeah, I know. A couple months ago I had a total space cadet moment and DREW in a library book. That went over like a turd in a punch bowl.

"Nate," she says, "people are different. Some are neat, and others are messy."

Yes, and some enjoy listening to grown-ups flap

their gums, and others don't. Can we move on?

"But when being messy and careless affects other people or their belongings . . ."

"Problem" sounds so negative. How about "lovable quirk"?

"Lecture's over," she says, giving me one last hairy eyeball. "I'll let you get back to your meeting."

Francis and Teddy are on one of the computers. I pull up a chair.

I start to say "nothing," but who am I kidding? I can't keep secrets from the guys. I give them a recap of my one on one with Ol' Silent but Deadly.

"No," I remind him. "You told me I was a PIG!"

"A SLOB, not a pig," Francis corrects me.

"Slob. Pig. Let's compromise!" Teddy says . . .

"Alphabetizing all the portraits," Francis says. "Some of these are a RIOT!"

"Here's Randy!"

"He looks like he's about to throw up."

"You'd throw up, too, if you looked like Randy."

"Lights! . . . Camera! . . . Dee Dee!"

"That smile is so fake."

"Good thing she flossed that day."

"Yikes. Check out the zit on Artur!"

"Wait, IS that a zit?"

"Um, it's either a zit or a small island."

"Let's find YOUR picture, Nate!" Francis grins.

"Let's not," I answer quickly.

Teddy's busting a gut. "Oh, MAN! I'd forgotten how BAD your picture turned out!"

Yeah, because it didn't happen to YOU, that's why. Trust me, I remember it just FINE. It was another episode of . . .

My name's Nate, what's... OOPS!
! ! !
SPLOOSH!
GASP!
HA HA HA HA HA
HA HA HA HA HA HA
HA HA HA HA
HA HA HA HA
HA HA HA
HA HA
HA HA
HA HA HA HA
THEN, at that very moment...
Students with last names beginning with V or W... report to the gym for school pictures.
GAH!
I can't get my picture taken wearing THIS!
The kids in my group were all GIRLS...
...so I can't borrow any of THEIR shirts!

Luckily, the School Picture Guy came to the rescue... OR SO I THOUGHT!
Never fear, kid!
I've got you covered!
SMILE
I have an EXTRA SWEATER for just such an emergency!
Put this on, m'boy!
Okay.
Seconds later...
Uh... this sweater is kind of...
Say CHEESE, champ!
WAIT! I'M NOT READY!
NEXT!
KLIK!

Ta-da. There it is: the lamest picture in the history of the school. Maybe in the history of the UNIVERSE.

"Wow," Teddy gasps, picking himself up off the floor. "And I thought joining the yearbook committee was going to be BORING!"

"Shut up," I grumble.

"Oh, don't take it so seriously, Nate," Francis says.

Yeah, he's right. I just hate looking like such a dweeb. I'd much rather be . . .

"Candids!" I say to Francis and Teddy as we leave the yearbook meeting.

"It's a picture you take of someone when they don't know you're taking it," Francis explains.

"Now that you mention it," says Francis, rubbing his chin in a co-editor-of-the-yearbook sort of way, "last year's Chronicle had almost NO candids!"

"Yet another reason it stank on ice," Teddy says.

Hey, LOOK, everybody: It's NICK BLONSKY, here to share all his yearbook expertise! No offense, Nick, but isn't that like the captain of the "Titanic" offering to give sailing lessons?

"Oh, it stank, all right," Teddy tells him.

"Those mistakes weren't MY fault," Nick whines.

Ugh. See that? Nick spits when he talks. Every time he says a "P" word, he practically floods the hallway. Anybody got a towel?

Nick snorts so hard, he blows a little snot bubble out of his nose. That's SO nasty.

"Good LUCK!" he sneers. "There's no such thing as a mistake-free yearbook!"

"How nice of him to offer a few words of encouragement," Francis says, rolling his eyes.

"What a dorkus maximus," Teddy grumbles.

"Forget about him, you guys," I tell them.

You're probably thinking: WHAT?? Since when do I go LOOKING for she-who-must-not-be-named? Especially since she's been on a total rampage lately.

"Okay, I'm stumped," Teddy says. "WHY are we going to see Mrs. Godfrey?"

"Because she's in charge of the audiovisual room," I explain. "I need to borrow one of the school's cameras . . ."

Francis gives me one of those are-you-crazy? looks.

"Dream ON, Nate! Those cameras are only for TEACHERS!"

"Uh-huh." I nod. "Teachers ANNNNND . . ."

"She'll let YOU borrow a camera, Francis!" I point out. "She LIKES you! She REALLY likes you!"

"No, what she LIKES is the fact that I don't do stupid things!" he answers.

"That may have been a mistake," I admit.

"You're ALWAYS making 'mistakes'!" Francis says, curling his fingers into air quotes. "What if I put myself on the line and borrow the camera . . ."

Teddy chuckles and gives me a shove. "You DO have a way with food!"

Francis is still babbling. "The bottom line is: If you break the camera . . ."

"I'm not going to break it," I object.

". . . or ruin it somehow . . ."

"I'm NOT going to RUIN it!"

Just the THOUGHT of getting in trouble gives Francis a stress rash. "Listen, that'll NEVER happen," I tell him. "I SWEAR."

I guess I should explain what a "secret swear" is. It's like a pact between me and Francis. Back in third grade we were already best friends, but we wanted to make it official. So we climbed into Francis's tree house and wrote this out:

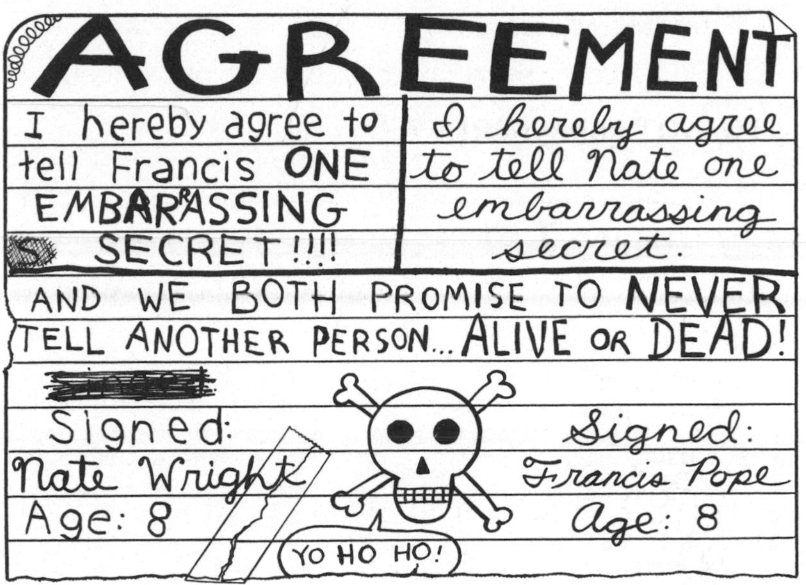

Who knows why we put a skull and crossbones on it. I guess we were in a pirate phase.

Anyway, I told him my biggest secret, and he told me his. And, no, I won't let you know what we said.

We've never told anyone. Not even TEDDY. It's a pretty big deal. This sounds kind of cheesy, but it's basically saying that you trust someone with ANYTHING. A secret swear is way more than a promise. It's a stone-cold LOCK.

Francis takes a deep breath. "Okay," he says finally. "I'll go ask Mrs. Godfrey for the camera. But stay out of sight, Nate."

"He's right," says Teddy matter-of-factly. "Mrs. Godfrey hates you."

Teddy snickers. "Well . . ."

"Don't answer that," I say quickly.

From around the corner, we hear a door open. Mrs. Godfrey's voice comes floating up the hallway.

A few seconds later, here comes Francis—WITH the camera!

"You GOT it!" I exclaim. "Lemme see!"

"Let's wait 'til we get outside," Francis whispers.

We step out into the school yard, and Francis hands over the camera. It's in a leather case, and there's a tag on the strap that says "Property of P.S. 38." How fancy can you get?

"You heard what Mrs. Godfrey said, right?" Francis asks. "About it being expensive?"

"Yes. RELAX, will you?" I tell him. "All I'm going to do is take a few pictures!"

Great. It's Randy Betancourt and his band of Merry Morons. As usual, he's acting like a total slimeball.

"Give it back," I growl.

Randy just smirks.

What can we do? If Randy were just one guy, the three of us could take the camera back. But he's NEVER just one guy. And we're no match for his whole posse.

"It's not a PURSE, butthead," Teddy says.

Randy opens his mouth to speak, but then . . .

Coach John walks by.
He hasn't seen us yet . . .
but he MIGHT. Randy nods at his buddies, and they quickly form a wall to block him from Coach John's view. So much for the whole teacher-to-the-rescue thing.

Randy and his posse scatter. I watch in horror as the leather case soars into the sky. In about five seconds, that camera's going to smash into a million pieces on the pavement—unless it doesn't HIT the pavement. I start running.

I'VE GOT TO MAKE THE GREATEST CATCH EVER...
...OR ELSE!

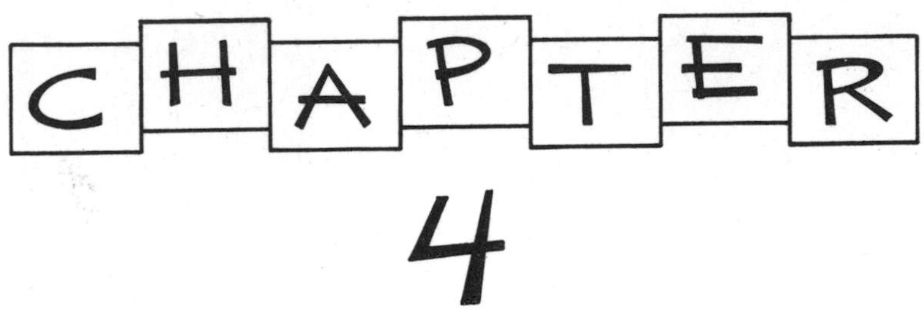
CHAPTER
4

THE PATHETIC MISADVENTURES OF...
RANDY BUTTANCOURT,
6TH GRADE* ~~BULLY~~ MORON!
*NOTE: He SHOULD be in 7TH grade, but he flunked kindergarten!
I did NOT flunk kindergarten!
I flunked PRESCHOOL!
SHOVE!
mystery guest star!
TODAY'S EPISODE: "CAMERA CRAZY"

Earlier today in the school yard...
I'm such a LOSER!
Everyone hates me!
Even WE hate you, and we're your POSSE!
Hey, I know! I'll BULLY someone to feel BETTER about myself!
Good plan, Randy!
Oh HO! THERE'S a likely victim!
WHAT?
But that's NATE WRIGHT! He's COOL! And he's TOUGH!
Don't try it, Randy! You're no match for HIM!

No problem. I'M a total wuss-pot, but YOU guys can protect me!
Besides, I want to check out that swanky CASE he's carrying!
tippy-toe tippy-toe
I'LL take that!
Huh?
NAB!
HAW! GOT it!
Randy, LOOK!
It's COACH JOHN!
Uh-oh!
Better get rid of the EVIDENCE!
FLING!!

YAAH! RANDY THREW THE CAMERA!!
EGAD!
THIS is a job for...
... ULTRA-NATE!
RRIIIIIP!
Even with my TURBO-SPEED, I won't reach it before it SMASHES on the ground!
TELESCOPIC VISION!
There's only one chance: my SUPER SUCTION BREATH!
Like a giant vacuum cleaner, Ultra-Nate INHALES...
HOOOOOO

...and the camera case is drawn into the ULTRA-VORTEX!
ZZZZZZZIP!
THAT WAS AMAZING!
I swallowed a few bugs, but it was WORTH it!
Uh-oh! I'd better SCRAM!
HEY! RANDY'S ESCAPING!
Not on MY watch!
FOOM!

"Very interesting," Dad says over my shoulder, and I almost jump out of my jammies. Doesn't anybody ever KNOCK around here?

"The part where I'm wearing tights and flying through the air is made up," I tell him.

"Got it." He chuckles, and sits down on the bed. Oh, yippee. Looks like Dad's in one of his tell-me-everything-about-your-life moods.

"Did Randy really get detention?"

I snort. "Are you kidding?"

"And that's coming from an authority on the subject," Dad says. But not in a mean way. He's just busting my chops a little bit.

"So what DID happen?" he asks.

WELL, RANDY CHUCKED THE CAMERA WAY UP IN THE AIR...

"... and it wasn't like there was anyplace SOFT for it to land. So I bombed across the school yard. I've never run that fast in my whole LIFE."

"And did you catch it?" Dad asks.

"I was ABOUT to," I grumble. "It was going to be the most amazing catch of all time. Then Kim Cressly got in my way."

"Who's Kim Cressly?"

"Just some girl," I say quickly. No way I'm telling Dad that Kim wants me to be her love puppet. Parents get all weird about that stuff.

"Anyway," I continue, "while I was trying to . . . uh . . . get past Kim, guess who came bumbling along: NICK BLONSKY! And then . . ."

"Let me guess," Dad says. "Nick caught it."

I nod in disgust. "Yes, and believe me, that was a total MIRACLE. He was on my SPOFF flag football team last fall . . ."

"Well, at least the camera wasn't broken," Dad notes.

"EXACTLY! That's what I told him! But he STILL laid this huge LECTURE on me!"

Dad notices the case next to my bed and opens it.

"Wow," he exclaims. "This IS a nice camera."

"Uh-huh," I agree. "And starting tomorrow, I'll be using it to shoot some KILLER candids!"

"Well, 'Killer,' there's more to being a yearbook photographer than playing Gotcha," he says. "Now go to sleep. It's getting late." He turns to leave.

On the walk to school the next morning, the guys and I talk strategy.

"Chester fell asleep in there last week, and he was drooling all over the beanbag chair!" Teddy laughs.

"Now THAT would have made a great candid!"

"If Chester caught you taking his picture, he'd probably kill you," Francis points out.

"Right," Francis says, rolling his eyes. "I forgot I was talking to a master photographer."

"What was THAT supposed to mean?" I ask the guys. "I haven't even TAKEN any pictures yet!"

Teddy points at the bulletin board. "Uh . . . I think they were talking about THAT one."

"That—that's ME!" I sputter.

"Brilliant observation," Francis deadpans.

Gina. I should have known.

"You think you're funny, Gina?" I snap.

"The 'big idea' was to let people know about Retake Day, genius," she says.

"How, by plastering my picture all over the school?"

"Oh, RELAX," she huffs. "You're on ONE POSTER."

She pulls some sheets from under her arm. "I used plenty of OTHER pictures, too. Look."

"See?" she says with an innocent little grin. "A whole BUNCH of us made posters!"

"That's DIFFERENT! You used my REAL school portrait! THOSE are FAKE!" I shout. "You were trying to look dorky ON PURPOSE!"

"Yes." She smirks . . .

Behind me, Teddy snickers. Remind me to noogie him later.

"Take it down if you want." Gina shrugs. "But if you're so INSECURE that you can't poke fun at yourself . . ."

"I can poke fun at myself just fine," I mutter. "I just don't like when SHE does the poking."

"So what are you gonna do?" Teddy asks.

I open my backpack and pull out the camera. "I have an idea. It's still a little fuzzy . . ."

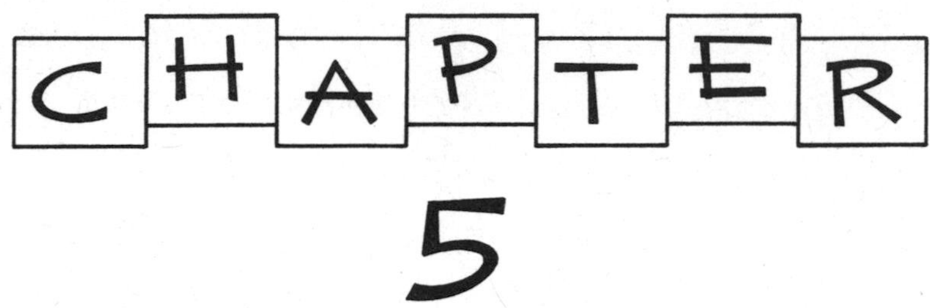

CHAPTER 5

"Skippy has $20. He buys four bags of tortilla chips to bring to Pepper's party. Each bag costs $2.60. Sales tax is 5 percent. How much money does Skippy have left?"

I hate problems like this. Plus, what's up with these stupid NAMES? "Pepper" sounds more like a HORSE than a person. And the only Skippy I've ever known was that labradoodle that used to poop every day in Francis's mom's garden.

Uh-oh. I feel a yawn coming on. And that's never a good idea during math.

First, Mr. Staples gets a little squirrelly if you look even a tiny bit bored.

And second, your best friend might almost KILL

you by choosing exactly the wrong moment to toss you a note.

"Nate!" Mr. Staples jumps up from his desk. "Are you all right?"

I quickly spit out the note and stuff it into my pocket. "Yeah, I'm okay," I tell him.

"Why don't you go drink some water," he suggests.

Not a bad idea. I'll get a two-minute break from Skippy and Pepper, AND I'll get to read this note that I halfway choked on.

I step into the hallway and fish the note from my pocket. It's a little moist. But readable.

Hmmph. Not so hot, that's how. My target isn't cooperating.

"O.C." stands for Operation Candid. It's my plan to get even with Gina for that little stunt she pulled. She wants to put a goofy-looking picture of me on a poster? Fine.

There's just one minor problem: I don't HAVE a goofy-looking picture of Gina. And I can't seem to GET one, either, because . . . well, this will explain why.

BUT no matter where she went, and no matter how many pictures I took...
KLIK!
INSIDE THE BRAIN
LIBRARY
CAFETORIUM
WAR AND PEACE
SCHOOL YARD
ROCKET SCIENCE
HALLWAY
...they all look EXACTLY THE SAME!

See what I mean? Gina just doesn't do goofy things. I always knew she was obnoxious. But until now, I didn't realize how BORING she is.

Hey, now THAT'S friendly. I come right back at him. "What are YOU doing here?"

He puffs out his chest.

Sounds about right. Hall monitors are dorks.

"You're SUPPOSED to be in class." A spray of Nick spit flies everywhere. "I could REPORT you."

I brush past him and stalk back into the math room, slamming the door behind me. Whoops. That was kind of loud.

"If you're feeling better, Nate, please resume your work," Mr. Staples says.

"The CAMERA?" Teddy says in disbelief.

"It's here somewhere," I assure him as my heart starts pounding through my chest. But it's NOT here somewhere. With my palms turning sweaty, I paw through the pile again. And again. I'm in full panic mode now.

Then I hear Francis behind me.

"What?" I ask. My voice sounds faraway.

"You lost the camera," Francis says.

"What's the matter?" Teddy whispers as I flop back into my seat. "Your EARS!"

NATE FACT:
My ears turn bright red when I get mad.

I roll my eyes and wave him off. There's no need to tell him what a weasel Nick is. He already knows. EVERYBODY does.

I slog through the rest of math—in case you were wondering, Skippy has exactly $9.08 left—and then, just as the bell rings at the end of the period, things start looking up for Operation Candid.

"Did you hear that, guys?" I exclaim as we file out of class. "Here's my big chance!"

Teddy looks confused. "To jump rope?"

"She's about as graceful as a rock in a blender!" I continue. "I bet I can get some GREAT shots of her looking like a total DOOFUS!"

"What's the matter?" Francis asks.

"Nothing, nothing," I answer, my tightening. "It's just that . . ."

"What's the matter?" Teddy whispers as I flop back into my seat. "Your EARS!"

I roll my eyes and wave him off. There's no need to tell him what a weasel Nick is. He already knows. EVERYBODY does.

I slog through the rest of math—in case you were wondering, Skippy has exactly $9.08 left—and then, just as the bell rings at the end of the period, things start looking up for Operation Candid.

"Did you hear that, guys?" I exclaim as we file out of class. "Here's my big chance!"

Teddy looks confused. "To jump rope?"

"She's about as graceful as a rock in a blender!" I continue. "I bet I can get some GREAT shots of her looking like a total DOOFUS!"

"What's the matter?" Francis asks.

"Nothing, nothing," I answer, my throat tightening. "It's just that . . ."

"The CAMERA?" Teddy says in disbelief.

"It's here somewhere," I assure him as my heart starts pounding through my chest. But it's NOT here somewhere. With my palms turning sweaty, I paw through the pile again. And again. I'm in full panic mode now.

Then I hear Francis behind me.

"What?" I ask. My voice sounds faraway.

"You lost the camera," Francis says.

"No, I didn't, I just—"

He nods his head. "Yes, you did, Nate. Just admit it. You lost the camera . . ."

"I DID NOT lose it!" I protest. "I'm . . ."

"Oh? Then WHERE IS IT?" he snaps.

"I . . . it's . . ." I stammer.

"You can't answer!" Francis says, his voice rising. "You have NO IDEA where it is!"

I can feel my ears starting to burn. Francis isn't being fair. It's not like I left the camera lying on the GROUND somewhere. It was in my locker. I KNOW it was!

FRANCIS. CALM DOWN. I **WAS** CAREFUL. I...

"No, you WEREN'T!" Francis explodes. "This is so TYPICAL, Nate! You always screw up, and then I'M the one who has to FIX everything!"

Now I'm mad. "Well, we can't all be PERFECT like YOU, can we?" I say bitterly.

"I never SAID I was perfect!" he yells.

It's like getting punched in the face. Francis has called me a loser before. But not like this. Not like he really MEANS it. I can feel my answer rising in my throat. Before I even know what I'm saying, before I can stop myself, I open my big, fat mouth.

Silence. For the first time, I notice the crowd. Half the school's been listening. And they

just heard me break the promise I made to Francis in third grade.

I told them his secret.

A few people laugh along with Randy. Other kids seem stunned. Francis looks pale. He opens his mouth for a second, then closes it. He shakes his head. Then he turns away.

I catch up to him. He doesn't stop walking.

"H-hey," I stutter.

"I shouldn't have . . . I didn't . . ." My voice trails off. I can barely talk.

I start again. "Francis," I say, forcing the words out. "I . . . I made a mistake."

He doesn't even look at me. "So did I," he says.

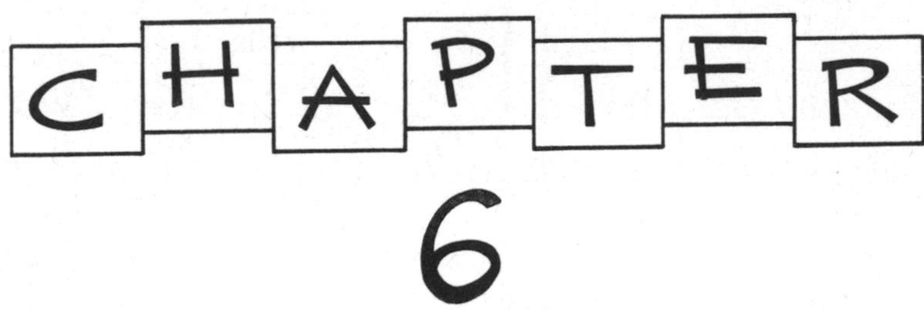
CHAPTER
6

He's HOT on the trail... of HILARITY!
LUKE WARM, PRIVATE EYE!
One fine day...
UKE WARM
Gooood morning, Miss Terry!
Good morning, Luke.

Got any "impossible" cases for me to solve? chuckle!
Nope.
No murders?
No.
No kidnappings?
No.
How about a really hard sudoku?
No.
DARN it! There's never any CRIME around here!
What's WRONG with this town?
SUDDENLY!
RRINNG!
What? At the MIDDLE SCHOOL, you say?
I'll be RIGHT OVER!
Soon...
SCREEE
WHAM!
SCHOOL ZONE

What a stupid place for a sign!
Soon...
So the camera was in your LOCKER?
Yes, and then it was GONE!
me
I've GOT it! Maybe the camera was... STOLEN!
You think?
AH-HA! HEY! YOU!
SURRENDER, YOU FIEND!!
WHUMP!

I've captured the thief!
WHAT? That's no THIEF!
But... he has a CAMERA!
Because he's the SCHOOL PICTURE GUY, you nimrod!
He wasn't even HERE the day the camera disappeared!
Oopsy. My bad.
The REAL thief must've been someone who KNEW I had the camera!
...maybe even somebody who tried to steal it once before!
HEY!
! ! !
THAT'S IT!

Yeah, that IS it! Why didn't I think of it BEFORE?

Dee Dee flops down next to me.

"I just figured out who stole that camera from my locker!" I tell her.

Then Dee Dee starts nodding like a dashboard bobblehead. "It sounds like the sort of mondo jerko thing he'd do. . . .

. . . But how can you prove it?"

"I'm not sure," I admit. "Maybe just by following him around. Spying on him."

I'm about to tell Dee Dee that the whole point of being a spy is NOT to be noticed, when . . .

We walk in silence—which NEVER happens when Dee Dee's around—but after a few minutes, she can't resist saying something.

Just hearing Francis's name makes my stomach hurt. I don't really want to go there, but Dee Dee's going to keep asking until I spill my guts. So why not? Maybe I'll feel better.

Dee Dee waggles her finger at me. "Never say never, Nate! Sure, Francis is upset NOW . . ."

"Except it's about more than just the camera," I remind her.

"Yes, I know, the whole 'Butthurst' thing," Dee Dee says, waving her hand impatiently.

"Like what?"

"Like mine," she answers. "It's Dorcas."

I snicker. "Sorry. I'm picturing a gazelle named Dorcas."

Good ol' Teddy. At least HE's not mad at me.

He claps his hands once, then rubs them together. "So!" he says. "What are we gonna do?"

"About what?" I ask.

"About YOU AND FRANCIS, fool!" he answers.

I hadn't really thought of that. It's probably no fun for Teddy to be stuck in the middle.

Teddy nods. "Just a couple minutes ago. He was on his way to tell Mrs. Godfrey about the camera."

There's no mistaking Mrs. Godfrey's voice. It sounds like a head-on collision between a foghorn and a chain saw. Teddy, Dee Dee, and I sneak down the hall toward her classroom to listen in.

Francis isn't easy to hear. "I . . . um . . . can't remember. I must have . . . misplaced it."

There's a pause, then Mrs. Godfrey's voice booms again. "This doesn't sound like you, Francis. Are you sure YOU lost the camera? . . ."

I brace myself. Here it comes. Here's where Francis tells her the whole story.

"He didn't rat you out!" Teddy whispers. "What a PAL!"

"Yeah," I mumble, feeling worse than ever.

Mrs. Godfrey gives a long sigh. I can practically smell her onion breath from here.

I wince. Hearing that from a teacher will cut Francis to the bone.

"You have detention for one week," Mrs. Godfrey continues. "And if the camera doesn't turn up during that time, you will pay the school the cost of replacing it."

"Yes, ma'am," Francis says quietly.

"You may go," she tells him.

"Guess he's still mad at you," Teddy says sadly.

"Poor Francis!" Dee Dee cries.

"I'm going to do more than that," I mutter.

Teddy looks baffled. "What do you mean?"

"Francis said it yesterday: I always screw up, and then he has to fix everything."

"People can't just change by snapping their fingers," Teddy scoffs.

Dee Dee's face lights up like a Christmas tree. "Not unless they're HYPNOTIZED!"

All three of us speak at once.

Teddy's uncle Pedro is . . . well, it's hard to describe him. He's sort of an inventor-magician-handyman-mad scientist sort of guy.

Oh, yeah. And he hypnotizes people.

UNCLE PEDRO'S GREATEST HYPNO-HITS!
#1 He helped Dee Dee's father lose FORTY-FIVE POUNDS!
...And when I clap my hands, you will find the taste of chicken-fried steak REPULSIVE!
'Kay.
#2 He cured Mrs. Godfrey of her chronic INSOMNIA!
ZZZZONK!
Can you keep her asleep until summer vacation?
#3 After only two sessions with Uncle Pedro, Chad's parakeet no longer uses inappropriate language!
SQUAWK! Gee whillikers!
I don't even KNOW you anymore!

No, I've never been hypnotized. But with the camera missing in action and Francis giving me the silent treatment, it might be my only hope. When school ends, the three of us make a beeline for Uncle Pedro's house.

"Uncle Pedro," Teddy says, "you remember my friends Nate and Dee Dee."

"Absolutely," he says, shaking our hands. He peers at me through his Coke-bottle glasses.

"Yeah, you're RIGHT!" I exclaim. "How'd you know that?"

"Lucky guess," he says simply. "Come inside."

"I was . . . uh . . . wondering if you could make me neater," I say after we sit down.

So I tell Uncle Pedro all about Francis and the camera and everything. Then I wait for him to put some crazy hypno-whammy on me. But he just reaches behind his back, winks at me, and says . . .

Huh? Is he serious? How's a CARD TRICK going to help?

"Any card," he says, nodding at me.

I don't get it. I was expecting him to wave a watch in my face or something. But I guess I've got nothing to lose. I slide a card from the deck and place it facedown on the table.

"Interesting," Uncle Pedro says. "Flip it over again."

I turn the card facedown.

"Your card was the seven of spades, correct?"

"Uh-huh," I answer.

"Hey, how'd you do that??" I ask in astonishment. "How'd you change it?"

"Me? YOU'RE the one who flipped the card over."

Uncle Pedro shrugs. "Then perhaps there is no explanation," he says.

Okay, I get it. It's a card trick. You're not SUPPOSED to know how it works. Let's move on.

"Can we start now?" I ask Uncle Pedro.

He shoots me a quizzical look. “Start what?”

“Well,” I say, a little confused. “Aren’t you going to hypnotize me?”

Uncle Pedro smiles.

7

"What a rip-off!" I grumble as we leave Uncle Pedro's.

"You don't feel any different?" Dee Dee asks.

"Not a bit," I snort.

Teddy frowns. "Since when are you afraid of a PUDDLE?"

"I'm not AFRAID of it, doofus," I answer.

"Are you CRAZY, Dee Dee?" I shout angrily. "YOU JUST RUINED MY SHIRT!"

"No, I just PROVED A POINT!" she says, grinning like the village idiot.

"NEAT? Open your EYES! I'm a MESS, thanks to you and your little MUD BALL attack!" I growl.

"You never cared about clean clothes BEFORE!" Teddy exclaims. "I think Dee Dee's right! You're HYPNOTIZED!"

"We need to make sure of it!" Dee Dee announces. "Let's do another test!"

"No more mud balls," I say quickly.

Mr. McTeague is a total whack job about his lawn. No, wait. He's a total whack job, PERIOD. What else do you call a guy who digs crabgrass out of his yard with a pair of eyebrow tweezers?

Teddy sweeps his arm across the bright green grass. "It's PERFECT, don't you think?"

Maybe I just never looked at Mr. McTeague's lawn all that carefully before. But I am now. And it's definitely got issues.

"Did you really just say the ACORNS are too messy?" Teddy asks in disbelief.

"I'm just pointing out they could be a bit more organized," I explain.

Dee Dee's hopping up and down like a frog on a pogo stick. "EUREKA! That PROVES it!!"

"Wow," I say as Dee Dee goes skipping away. "SOMEBODY'S pretty fired up about this."

"Well, aren't YOU?" Teddy asks.

And speaking of underwear, I've been wearing the same pair of tighty-whities since this morning. That's gross.

Dad's burning something on the stove when I walk through the kitchen door. "Hi, Nate! Want a snack? Supper won't be ready for a while."

"No, thanks. I've got some work to do in my room."

I'VE GOT SOMETHING MORE IMPORTANT TO DO!

A couple hours later, Dad knocks on my door.

Dad's lips start moving, but no sound comes out. Either he doesn't know what to say, or he just won a scholarship to mime school.

"Y-you cleaned your room," he finally stammers.

Brilliant observation, Dad. "Yeah," I tell him.

"With my hands. Because it was messy," I explain. Gotta love these father-son chats. They're so DEEP.

Downstairs at the supper table, Ellen continues the sparkling conversation.

"Besides an annoying big sister, you mean?" I ask.

"You've got your napkin in your lap for once,"

she says. "You haven't spilled anything yet. And you're actually CHEWING your food . . ."

" . . . a concept you're obviously too BRAIN-DEAD to understand!"

"You know what I think?" Dad announces in that fake-happy voice he uses whenever he's trying to keep Ellen and me from killing each other.

"No, thanks," I say as I put my dishes in the sink and head upstairs.

Later, Dad pokes his head in my room again.

"I don't," I tell him. "I'm just rewriting my class notes for social studies."

He sits down on my bed, which totally messes up

the blanket. But whatever. I'll fix it later.

"So this isn't something Mrs. Godfrey TOLD you to do?" he asks, as one of his eyebrows heads north.

"No, I just wanted to make them neater."

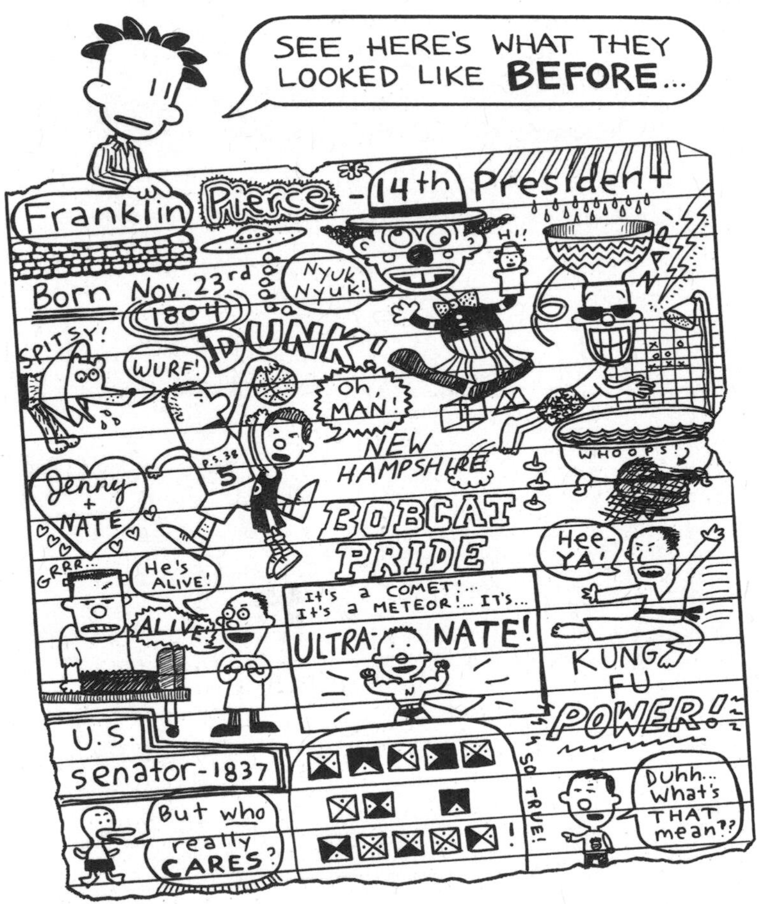

Class Notes
Social Studies

Nate Wright

Franklin Pierce - 14th President of U.S.

- Born Nov. 23rd, 1804 - Hillsboro, NH
  - parents: Anna Kendrick & Benjamin Pierce (governor of NH)
- 1824 - graduates from Bowdoin College
- 1829 - elected to NH legislature (becomes speaker in 1831)
- 1833 - elected to U.S. House of Reps.
- 1837 - begins first term as senator

Presidential Election of 1852

Franklin PIERCE (Democrat)	vs.	Winfield SCOTT (Whig)
50%	Popular Vote	44%
254	Electoral College	42

Pierce's Presidency

- Support for Kansas-Nebraska Act makes him unpopular in North
- Ostend Manifesto published

Dad hands me back my notes. He's got the weirdest expression on his face. It's like half worried, half gassy.

Hmm. Okay, here's where things get kind of dicey. I'm pretty sure Dad wouldn't be too happy about me getting hypnotized, so I can't tell him why I've turned into Joe Tidy. And if he finds out a camera disappeared from my locker, he's going to call the school. You never want a parent to call the school.

So I lie.

Dad gives me The Squint. He probably knows there's more to the story. But what can he do? Ground me for being too neat?

"Can I stay up and draw comics for a while?" I ask.

He smiles. "I suppose a miracle like that buys you some drawing time. But only half an hour, Nate. It's a school night."

"Thanks, Dad," I tell him. Then I jump into a

brand-new Luke Warm, Private Eye adventure. I'm just getting started when . . .

"What? You said I had a half hour!"

Dad taps his watch. "That WAS a half hour."

"But I haven't even started DRAWING yet! I barely finished measuring all the panels!"

I flail around for a good answer. "I just . . . I wanted all the panels to look nice and straight," I say weakly.

Dad peers down at my notebook. "Well, they certainly are nice and straight," he says.

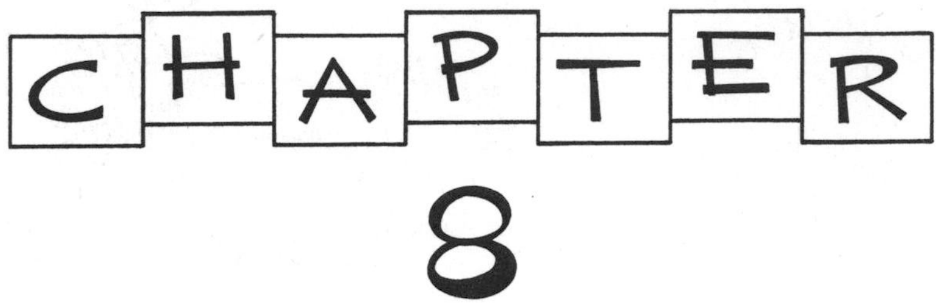

CHAPTER 8

The sun's barely up when I leave for school the next morning. I need to get there early . . .

He doesn't LOOK very sorry, if you ask me. But I'm so happy to see Francis, I don't even mind getting clocked in the face by . . . the "Daily Courier"?

He doesn't look at me. He won't even slow down. "I need the money," he says.

A hot wave of guilt washes over me—even though I have nothing to feel guilty about . . .

I guess I could chase after Francis and tell him that. AGAIN. Or I could tell him that he doesn't need to buy the school a new camera, that I'LL pay for it if I have to.

The school's pretty empty when I get there. And you know what? It looks GOOD this early.

Mrs. Hickson eyes me suspiciously—which makes sense, I guess. I'm usually here an hour AFTER school, not an hour before, if you get my drift.

"I want to clean my locker before homeroom," I answer.

Hickey looks like she might kiss me. (She doesn't. Phew.) "My goodness, Nate, this is WONDERFUL!" she gushes. "I assumed you'd LOST all these!"

"Nope!" I tell her. "I never lose stuff! . . ."

Or at least, I never USED to. But now that I've been hypnotized, I'm ready to send most of what's in my locker straight to Dump City.

It takes me almost forty-five minutes. What a disgusting job. You wouldn't believe all the stuff that comes out of there.

LOCKER INVENTORY
(not a complete list)

- 13 pairs of unwashed socks
- 3 molded (and moldy) plastic mouthguards
- 27 pencils
- 2 unfinished Dr. Cesspool comix
- 49 jelly beans
- ½ roll toilet paper
- 2 wooden drumsticks
- 2 chicken drumsticks
- 12.3 pounds of math homework
- 1 volleyball (deflated)
- 1 pair of Mr. Galvin's dentures
- 16 empty cheez doodle bags
- 1 sombrero
- the head of a lawn gnome
- 6⅓ cups of dirt

And I won't even get into how it SMELLED. Francis was right. I WAS a slob.

"I'm a SPY!" Dee Dee says, like it's supposed to be obvious. "That's how we TALK!"

"Where, at a BIRD SANCTUARY?" I say.

"No, silly!" She giggles.

"Here's a suggestion, 007," I whisper. "Don't announce to the world who you're about to spy on."

"Got it," Dee Dee says a little sheepishly.

Right. I'll believe it when I see it. Dee Dee's about as low-key as a match in a fireworks factory.

"Oh, and don't forget!" she calls over her shoulder.

My heart sinks. Oh, yeah. The Trivia Slam.

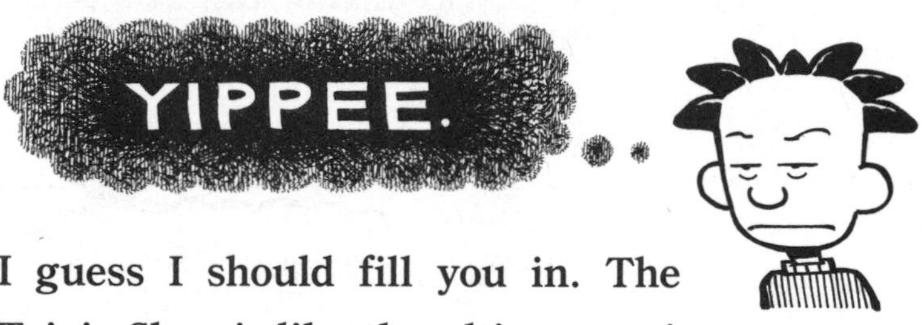

I guess I should fill you in. The Trivia Slam is like the ultimate quiz show. The questions can be about ANYTHING, and the last team standing wins. It happens every year, and it's HUGE.

I'm supposed to be on Francis's team—the Factoids—along with Teddy, Dee Dee, and Chad. Talk about a trivia powerhouse. As soon as we put that group together, we knew we had the goods to knock off the defending champs . . .

But everything's changed now. How can I be on the team . . .

When the bell rings for social studies, I'm still thinking about the Trivia Slam—until Mrs. Godfrey gets everyone's attention.

Translation: Get ready for Mrs. Godfrey to throw a conniption fit if she thinks your notebook is too sloppy. Or too unorganized. Or too red. On a normal day, a notebook check—for me, anyway—is a one-way ticket to detention.

But today's not a normal day.

Mrs. Godfrey's eyes look ready to pop out of their sockets as she flips through my notebook, staring at page after perfect page.

Five minutes with Uncle Pedro, that's what. But I just shrug my shoulders. "I decided I wanted to be neater, that's all," I say. Honest enough.

An A DOUBLE plus?? Holy COW!!

Isn't she charming? And so FRIENDLY, too. "There's no mystery, Gina: I've cleaned up my act."

This is killing her.

"Does it LOOK like I'm faking?" I ask. "Get used to the new me, Gina. Neatness is now my way of life."

HA! That's me one, Gina zero. And you want to know the best part? The rest of the day goes EXACTLY THE SAME WAY!

In English, Ms. Clarke gives me extra credit for my "phenomenal" penmanship. In math, Mr. Staples tells everybody my homework is the "Mona Lisa of bar graphs."

Even Old Fossil Face is impressed.

Not too shabby, right? As I head for my locker after class, I realize something: I didn't get yelled at today. Not even ONCE. Who knew it was this easy to make teachers happy?

Looks like Dee Dee's still in not-so-secret agent mode. "What's up?" I ask as I turn the corner.

"The pigeon has almost landed!" she whispers.

Not THIS again. "Try it in English, Dee Dee," I tell her. "I can't speak Spy."

"That DOES sound kind of suspicious," I admit, amazed that Dee Dee actually turned up some useful information.

"I'll continue my investigation tomorrow," she says.

That's good. The "bride of Dracula" look might not work two days in a row.

NOW C'MON, NATE! LET'S NOT KEEP OUR FELLOW FACTOIDS WAITING!

My stomach drops off a cliff. "You know what? I'm going to skip the Trivia Slam, Dee Dee. You guys will do fine without me."

"SURE, he does!" Dee Dee chirps a little too quickly.

"Oh, yeah?" I mutter. "Did you ask him?"

She gets a little fidgety. "I . . . I've talked to him about it a couple times, yes," she answers.

"Well? What did he say? In his EXACT WORDS."

"Uh . . ." Dee Dee mumbles nervously. "He said that . . . that he didn't care if you came or not."

"Francis didn't say you COULDN'T come! He just said that . . . um . . ."

I swallow the lump in my throat and start home.

They really WILL do fine without me. The Factoids, I mean. They can beat anybody, as long as they've got Francis. He's always been a trivia geek.

I come to the edge of the Little Woods. If I go to the left and stay on the sidewalk, I'll be home in ten minutes. But if I go to the right, there's a shortcut through the woods that leads straight to my street. It's a little muddy sometimes, but it's fast.

I go to the left.

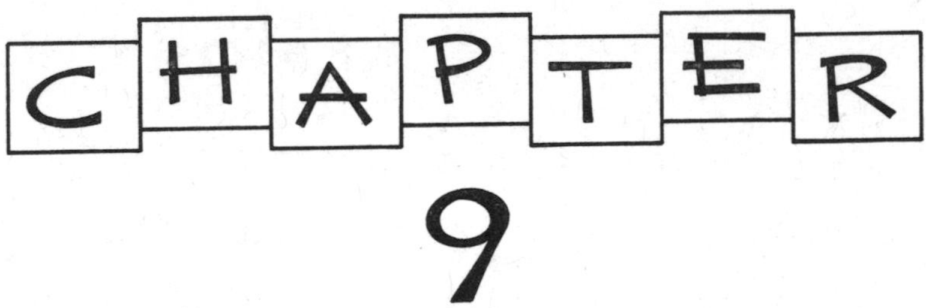

CHAPTER 9

I'm starting to hate being neat.

Everything takes so LONG. Like right now, for example. I'm getting ready for school picture Retake Day . . .

Pretty ridiculous, right? NOBODY spends that long on his hair.

But I can't help it. Whatever Uncle Pedro did when he hypnotized me is working TOO well.

Sure, there are some upsides to being a neatnik. Like my GRADES. All of a sudden, I'm getting A's in EVERYTHING.

Plus, I'm not spending my afternoons in detention. I haven't seen Mrs. Czerwicki for a WEEK.

But look, I didn't get hypnotized to be Joe Honor Roll. I did it to patch things up with Francis. Which isn't working out so hot.

And that's not all. Turning into Mr. Clean is ruining all my hobbies. I can't play soccer with the guys because—don't laugh—I'm worried about getting grass stains on my pants.

Oh, and want to read the latest edition of "Luke Warm, Private Eye"? Well, you CAN'T. I ripped it into a zillion pieces . . .

Huh? What does HE want? I'm used to Principal Nichols looking for me, but not with a SMILE on his face. It's a little creepy.

Okay, now it's a LOT creepy. Remember who ELSE

is a hall monitor? Nick Blonsky. Need I say more?

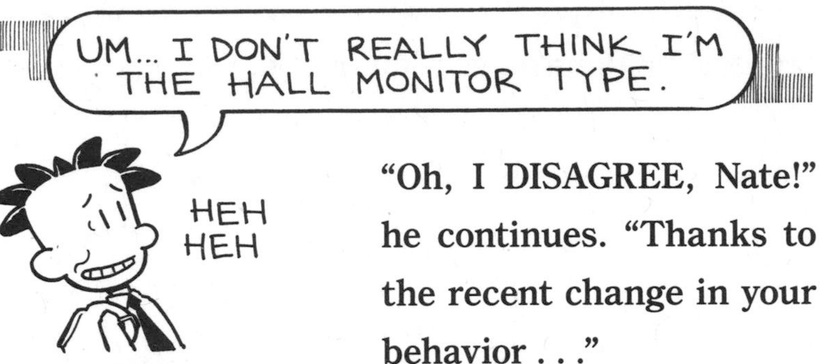

"Oh, I DISAGREE, Nate!" he continues. "Thanks to the recent change in your behavior . . ."

A BADGE? Why not just stamp "LOSER" on my forehead? It's pretty much the same thing.

"What do you mean?" I ask.

Teddy chuckles and tugs on my tie.

He'll WRINKLE it? LISTEN to me. I sound like a complete dorkwagon.

"Just don't TOUCH it," Teddy warns Dee Dee. "You might ruin Nate's swanky OUTFIT!"

"I never said that," I snap.

"You might as well have," Teddy growls.

Dee Dee jumps in. "Guys, GUYS!"

"That's just what I saw the other day!" Dee Dee whispers excitedly. "Randy's showing off the

CAMERA he stole from your locker, Nate!"

Teddy frowns. "How do you know?"

She shakes her head. "I don't, exactly."

"What's she talking about?" Teddy whispers.

I shrug. "Who knows? I try not to spend any time inside Dee Dee's head."

"Good point." Teddy snickers. "That's a weird neighborhood."

We watch as Dee Dee strolls casually over to Randy and his posse. Then . . .

She hits the floor like a sack of potatoes. Randy drops something. But it's not the camera.

I hear him angrily whisper to his friends as he stoops to the floor.

"Pick WHAT up? What ARE those?" Teddy asks.

"Beats me," I answer as Dee Dee climbs shakily to her feet.

"Well, go faint somewhere ELSE," Randy snarls.

Dee Dee wobbles away from Randy and his gang like a leaky balloon, then finds Teddy and me around the corner.

"What HAPPENED over there?" we both ask.

It's a Gag Me card. Those aren't allowed at P.S. 38. If you get busted with them, you're in big trouble.

"Well, that explains why Randy looked like he was hiding something," Teddy says.

I nod sadly. "Yeah. But it wasn't the camera."

"I'm beginning to think Randy's too STUPID to steal a camera." Dee Dee frowns. "Maybe someone ELSE took it."

Teddy heaves a sigh. "Maybe. But WHO?"

The bell rings. Time for homeroom.

"Let's talk more about it later, during our free period," Dee Dee suggests.

I shake my head. "It'll have to wait 'til lunch."

Which turns out to be as exciting as Mr. Galvin's rock collection. All you do is walk up and down the corridors. I feel like those old people who do laps around the mall.

It's Nick. But for a second, I almost don't recognize him. He's walking really fast, and he's all hunched over. I take another look, and . . . HEY!!

Or does he? He's too far away for me to tell for sure. But he's got SOMETHING tucked under his arm. And it sure LOOKS like the camera.

I take off after him.

You're not supposed to run in the hallways—ESPECIALLY if you're a hall monitor. But this is an emergency. I kick it into overdrive and round the corner. Then . . .

What idiot put a DESK here? I scramble off the floor, ready to crank up my Nick chase again.

He's already way ahead of me.
I can't waste another second.

Then I look around.

The old me wouldn't have worried about a few papers on the floor. I would have sprinted after Nick like a crazed bloodhound. If I'm going to get that stupid camera back, that's what I should do.

But I can't.

I start picking up all the sheets and stacking them on the desk. Not because I want to. Because I HAVE to. Being hypnotized leaves me no choice.

The lunch bell rings. The hallway fills up with people. Whatever chance I had to catch Nick red-handed is long gone.

What a mess.

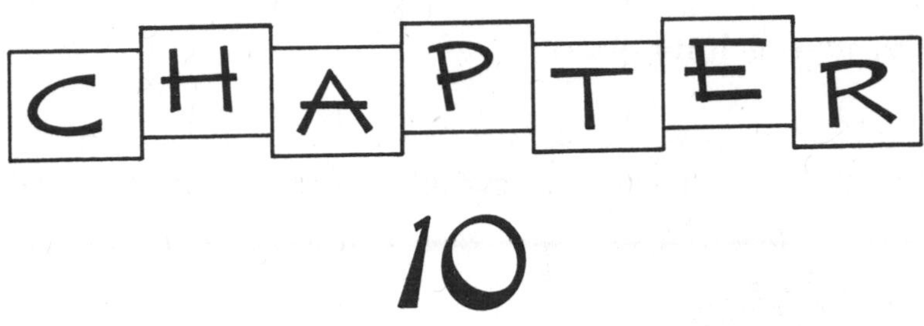

"I just had a chance to solve the camera mystery, and I BLEW it . . ."

I tell Teddy and Dee Dee about seeing Nick with the camera and how he got away.

Teddy rolls his eyes. “Funny how you never mentioned that, Sherlock.”

“I can’t take this anymore,” I say miserably.

"Sorry, dude." Teddy shakes his head. "Uncle Pedro's visiting my grandparents in Mexico. He'll be back in a week."

"I've heard that sometimes a DRAMATIC EVENT can snap a person out of a hypnotic trance!"

"What kind of dramatic event?"

Dee Dee sighs. "I don't know."

Okay, NOW we're talking. Cheez Doodles make everything better. And I'm STARVING. I didn't eat breakfast this morning because I was obsessing about my hair, remember? I reach into the bag.

"What's the matter?" Teddy asks.

"I got orange powder all over my hands."

He makes a tell-me-something-I-didn't-know face. "Well, DUH!"

"And so MESSY," I say, pushing the bag away.

Teddy's jaw drops.

Dee Dee gasps.

I know. And now they DISGUST me. I lay my head on the table (after wiping it off with Teddy's napkin) and try to pull myself together. Francis hates me. None of my hobbies are fun anymore. And I can't even eat my favorite food in the whole world.

I look across the cafetorium, and I feel like throwing up. This is my fault. I spilled the beans about Francis's middle name. I might as well have painted a bull's-eye on his back.

The blood starts pounding in my head. The lunchtime noises fade away, until all I can hear is Randy's voice and his stupid laugh as he aims another kick at Francis's butt. I stand up.

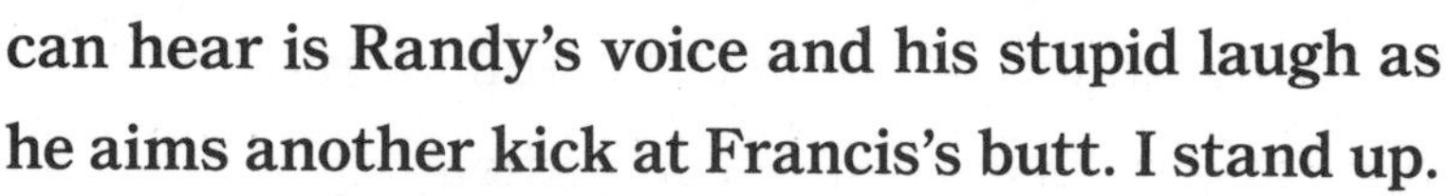

Then I flip out.

Okay, true confessions time: I've never been in a real fight before. So jumping on Randy like a rabid wolverine might not have been one of my better ideas. But it goes pretty well at first. In fact, I might actually be WINNING when . . .

"He ATTACKED me!" Randy whimpers, switching to victim mode in a millisecond.

Mrs. Czerwicki nods grimly. "I saw it."

"Not ALL of it," comes a familiar voice.

Mrs. C. looks surprised. "This really doesn't concern you, um . . . er . . ."

"Francis," he says helpfully.

"Yes, well, thank you for your input, Francis . . ."

Great. Nothing like a little quality time with the Big Guy. I won't bore you with the details. Basically, he yells at me. Nonstop. For about a half hour.

"Hey," says Francis.

"Oh. Uh . . . hey," I answer, trying to sound casual.

He nods toward the principal's office. "What did he say?"

"Just what I KNEW he'd say," I snort.

Francis shakes his head. "That's so bogus."

I shrug. "I guess I DID sort of ambush him. But he deserved it."

"Uh-huh. Probably the stupidest thing I've ever done."

"Why? I mean, it WORKED, obviously."

"Yeah, I'm neater than YOU are now," I tell him.

"That's unbelievable!" Francis exclaims. "Considering what it USED to look like, it's . . ."

But I've stopped listening. My eyes are locked on a leather case tucked alongside the textbooks on the top shelf.

I examine the case. It's definitely the same camera, right down to the "Property of P.S. 38" tag.

Francis is flabbergasted. "Wha—? How did . . . ? Nate, what's going on?"

"I'll tell you what's going on: NICK thinks he's being FUNNY."

"Nick BLONSKY?" Francis asks in surprise.

"What are you two doing out of class?" He smirks, flashing his hall monitor badge.

"Oh, nothing," I reply angrily.

He shrugs, pretending to be confused. "If I STOLE it, then how can YOU be holding it RIGHT NOW?"

"Because you put it back. During third period.

I saw you with it."

Another smirk. "Maybe you did, and maybe you didn't," he says in a singsong voice.

"Because it was HILARIOUS," Nick answers. "That FIGHT you two had when you realized the camera was gone was PRICELESS!"

What a twerp. I'm about two seconds away from

my SECOND fight of the day. “You’re a riot,” I snarl through gritted teeth.

“We could report you to Principal Nichols for this,” Francis adds.

“Dee Dee Holloway, super spy, at your service!” she says, taking a bow.

The tiniest look of uncertainty creeps across Nick’s face. “Super spy?”

Dee Dee smiles slyly. "You guys were having such an interesting conversation . . ."

Nick turns pale. He backs away from us, slowly at first. Then he breaks into a run.

I could hug Dee Dee. I don't, of course. But I COULD. "Dee Dee," I tell her gratefully, "that was . . . AWESOME!"

"Yup! The pigeon has landed!" she says, beaming.

Then she grabs me and Francis. "But HERE'S what's REALLY awesome!"

Well, if I didn't hug Dee Dee, I'm sure not going to KISS Francis. I stick out my hand. And so does he, at the exact same moment.

"I shouldn't have accused you of losing the camera," Francis says. "That was lame."

"And I shouldn't have told the whole school your

middle name," I admit. "That was lamer."

"This is FABULOUS!" Dee Dee squeals.

Then, with a gasp, Dee Dee turns me loose. "Nate! There's FOOD on your shirt!"

Makes sense. An hour ago, I was rolling around on the cafetorium floor with Randy. "So?" I ask her.

Suddenly it dawns on me what she's getting at.

Dee Dee's bouncing around like her hair's on fire. "Remember what I said? That a dramatic event might snap you out of it?"

I fling open my locker—my disgustingly neat locker—and grab a pencil and paper.

"If I can draw something without worrying how PERFECT it is, then we'll know I'm not hypnotized anymore!"

I go as fast as I can. No rulers. No erasing. And by the time I'm finished, I can tell I'm myself again. Because this definitely isn't perfect.

But it might be the most awesome drawing I've ever made.

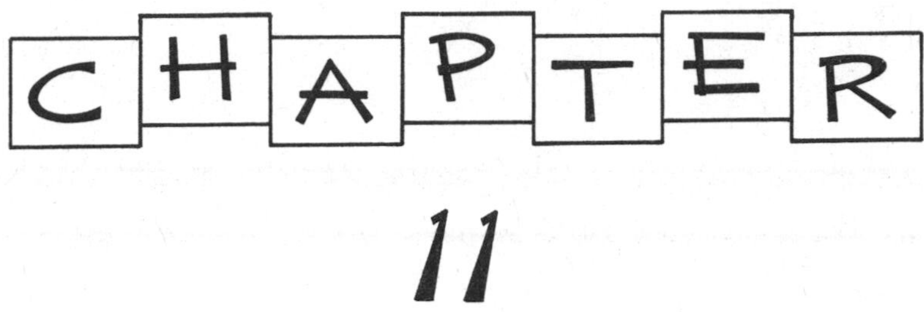

CHAPTER 11

Nick's not in school the next day. But we don't find out why until Francis, Teddy, and I walk into the Chronicle meeting after classes are over.

"Hold it," I say. "Nick gets to stay home from school? For a whole WEEK?"

That's WAY better than what I got. Principal Nichols gave me three days of detention for fighting with Randy. Then he called my dad. Guess what they talked about?

Ugh. Gina and her stinkin' gavel. Couldn't we start the meeting with something a little mellower? Like a foghorn?

"I've been working on some of these page layouts," Gina announces as we gather around the table. "The group shots look really good . . ."

"What are you trying to PULL, Gina?" Teddy demands angrily. "You only used pictures of YOURSELF and your snobby FRIENDS!"

"And besides, NATE was supposed to supply the candids!" Francis chimes in.

"I'm afraid I can't allow that, Gina," says a voice from behind us.

YES! Hickey to the rescue! Gina turns fire-engine red, then corkscrews her face into a phony smile.

"All right," she says, turning to Francis. "What do YOU want to do?"

Mrs. Hickson nods. "I think that's a fair solution. But, Nate, we DO have a deadline, so . . ."

"No problem!" I say immediately. "I should get PLENTY of good candids TOMORROW . . ."

The next morning as we walk to school, I realize two things: (1) it's great to be friends with Francis again, and (2) he's driving me completely insane.

"Nate's right," Teddy says. "You're going to fry your brain before the Trivia Slam even STARTS."

Francis takes a deep breath. "I know, I know."

They COULD. But I still think we'll smuck 'em.

FRANCIS'S FACTOIDS
VS.
GINA'S (SO-CALLED) GENIUSES
TEAM MEMBER
TRIVIA SPECIALTY
TRIVIA SPECIALTY
TEAM MEMBER
FRANCIS POPE
every-thing
every-thing
...and MORE!
GINA HEMPHILL-TOMS
NATE WRIGHT
comics, Ben Franklin, history of snack foods, Greek myths
science fiction, martial arts, video games
ERIC FLEURY
DEE DEE HOLLOWAY
art, drama, fashion, musical theater
NO INFO
? ? ? ?
TEDDY ORTIZ
sports, comedy, foreign languages, movie quotes
flute music, cosmetology, reality television
MARY ELLEN POPOWSKI
CHAD APPLEWHITE
breakfast, scouting, lunch, animals, dinner
computer science, math, law enforcement
NICK BLONSKY
SUSPENDED

The cafetorium's already mobbed when we get there. "I wonder who Gina will get to replace Nick," Teddy says as we squeeze through the door.

We don't have to wait long to find out.

Wait, did he say "whom"? That's SO Francis. Even when he's trash-talking, he uses good grammar.

Teddy's mouth gapes open. "Is he SERIOUS? Why would Gina put an idiot like RANDY on her team?"

"Randy's no Einstein, but he knows a TON of sports and movie trivia," Francis explains. "Gina's team didn't have anybody like that before."

Well . . . MAYBE. But there's no time to worry about it now. Ms. Clarke is asking for quiet and explaining the rules.

"You all know the format," she says. "During the preliminary rounds, you may consult your teammates before answering each question. But during the FINAL round . . ."

Shut up? THAT'S the best snappy comeback I've got? Definitely not up to my usual standards. I must be nervous.

"You heard Ms. Clarke, Factoids!" Dee Dee says as she reaches into her book bag.

Leave it to Dee Dee to bring costumes into this. But whatever. If wearing dorky hats is going to help us take down Gina's Geniuses, I'm all for it.

"The first question is for Amanda's Pony Posse," Ms. Clarke announces.

Pretty easy, right? That's how the Trivia Slam works. The early rounds are ALWAYS a cakewalk. But as the game goes on, the questions get harder.

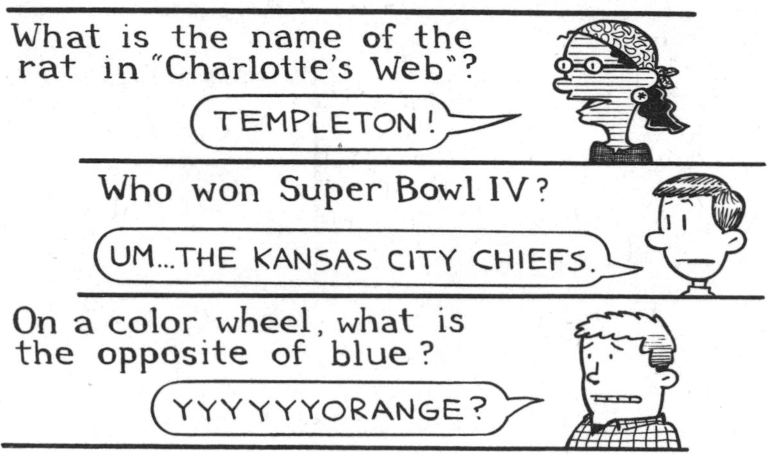

And the candids get better and better!

Teams start dropping like flies. Tricia's Tater Tots don't know the capital of Luxembourg. (Trick question. It's . . . Luxembourg.) Artur's Antelopes can't name the only vegetable that's also a flower. (Broccoli. Yuck.)

Eventually—just like everyone knew it would—it comes down to two teams.

"Okay, guys, here's where all our practicing pays off!" Dee Dee whispers. "Try to relax."

RELAX? I can't relax when we're going toe to toe with Gina and Randy. You think they're obnoxious NOW? If they beat us, we'll never hear the end of it.

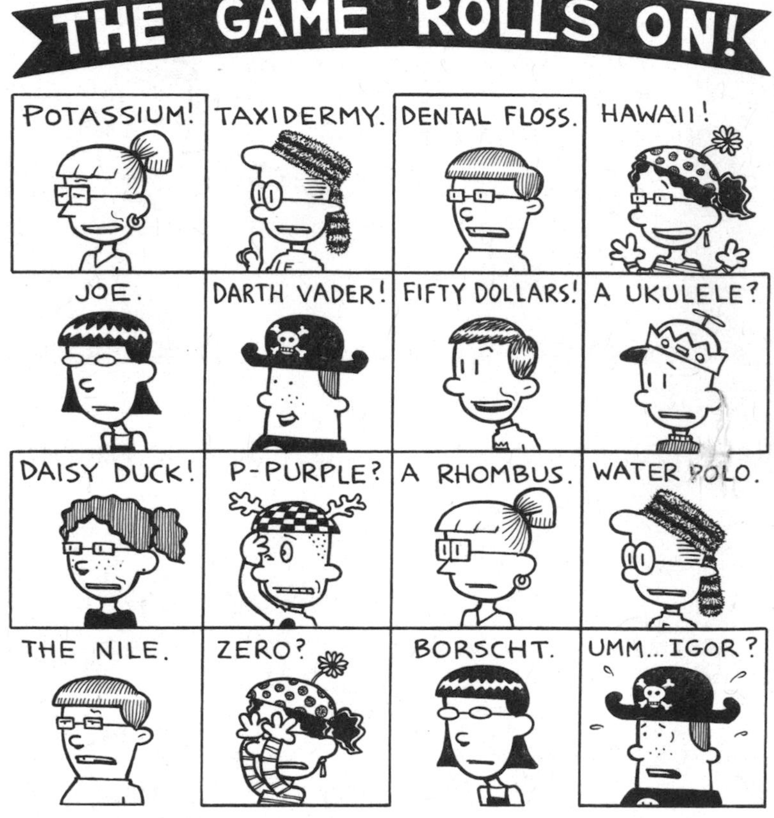

"Nice job, Chad!" I whisper as he steps down from the stage. He looks a little wobbly. The pressure's getting to everybody. And you know what they say about pressure: It breaks stuff. So who's going to crack first?

"Randy," Ms. Clarke says, "you're up."

Rats. A sports question. This'll be a no-brainer. Randy grins confidently.

At the beginning of a match, how many pawns are there on a chessboard?

The blood drains from his face. "W-wait a minute. CHESS? Chess isn't a SPORT!"

"It's recognized as a sport by the International Olympic Committee," Ms. Clarke states matter-of-factly. "Answer the question, please."

But Randy's not a chess player. He's more of a tic-tac-toe guy.

Remember, you can't ask your teammates for help in the final round. Randy's got to sink or swim on his own. And I've got a feeling . . .

Ms. Clarke shakes her head. "I'm sorry. The answer is sixteen. Eight per side."

Gina looks ready to wring Randy's neck, I'm snapping pictures as fast as I can, and Dee Dee's about to launch into the victory dance she's been rehearsing all week. But it's not over yet.

"If the Factoids answer the next question incorrectly, the game continues," Ms. Clarke says. "If they get it right, they're the champions."

I look over at Francis. He flashes me a gigantic smile. Why? Because he knows the same thing I do: We're about to win the Trivia Slam.

"That's correct." Ms. Clarke smiles. "Congratu—"

I don't hear the rest. Dee Dee wraps me in a bear hug, and a second later I'm on the bottom of a Factoid pig pile. Teddy's singing in Spanish, hats are flying everywhere . . . it's total pandemonium.

"I thought we were DOOMED when I heard that question!" Chad exclaims as we untangle ourselves.

Before I can answer, Francis slaps me on the shoulder. "He's just really good at trivia, that's all!"

But that's NOT all. And Francis knows it better than anybody.

See, that was my half of the friendship pact I made with Francis back in third grade. He told me his secret—Butthurst—and I told him mine: that I'm a complete cat coward. I know it sounds stupid, but cats just freak me out. They always have.

"Think of it this way," Francis says.

"Ooh! Guys! That reminds me . . ."

As the others scroll through the rest of the pictures, Francis and I step into the hall. "Hey, I just thought of something," he says. "Maybe Uncle Pedro could help you get over your cat phobia."

"No, thanks. Being hypnotized the first time didn't work out so hot."

He chuckles. "Yeah, I'm glad that didn't stick. I like you much better as a slob."

Hear that? Now THAT'S a best friend. We'll always be total opposites, but just because Francis is Mr. Clean, it doesn't mean he expects ME to be. He's happy with me just the way I am.

Lincoln Peirce

(pronounced "purse") is a cartoonist/writer and *New York Times* bestselling author of the hilarious Big Nate book series (www.bignatebooks.com), now published in twenty-seven countries worldwide and available as ebooks and audiobooks and as an app, Big Nate: Comix by U! He is also the creator of the comic strip *Big Nate.* It appears in over four hundred U.S. newspapers and online daily at www.gocomics.com/bignate. Lincoln's boyhood idol was Charles Schulz of *Peanuts* fame, but his main inspiration for Big Nate has always been his own experience as a sixth grader. Just like Nate, Lincoln loves comics, ice hockey, and Cheez Doodles (and dislikes cats, figure skating, and egg salad). His Big Nate books have been featured on *Today* and *Good Morning America* and in the *Boston Globe*, the *Los Angeles Times*, *USA Today*, and the *Washington Post*. He has also written for Cartoon Network and Nickelodeon. Lincoln lives with his wife and two children in Portland, Maine.

Also available as an ebook.

"ZONED" OUT!
You know what? Only a week ago, my life totally stunk.
ExCUSE me, but the CORRECT word would be "stank."
Okay, then— it STANK. Gina was being her usual know-it-all self...
Artur and Jenny were going overboard with the PDOs*...
nuzzle nuzzle
Ugh.
(*Public Displays of Obnoxiousness)
And worst of all: last week, REPORT CARDS got mailed home.
Ellen, I can't BELIEVE these GRADES!
Nate, I can't BELIEVE these grades.

Then—I'm not sure how, but it had something to do with Chad—my luck changed. Suddenly, I'm IN THE ZONE!
Congratulations, Nate! You're on the HONOR ROLL!
Hiiiiii, Nate!
SHOVE!
Nate, you made the league ALL-STAR TEAM!
I've NEVER had a hot streak like this before. The question is: HOW LONG WILL IT LAST??
Not very long!
"Big Nate is funny, big time." —Jeff Kinney, author of Diary of a Wimpy Kid
BIG NATE
IN THE ZONE
Lincoln Peirce
Maybe good luck isn't everything it's cracked up to be!
Read BIG NATE IN THE ZONE!

HE'LL TICKLE YOUR FUNNY BONE!

DOCTOR CESSPOOL

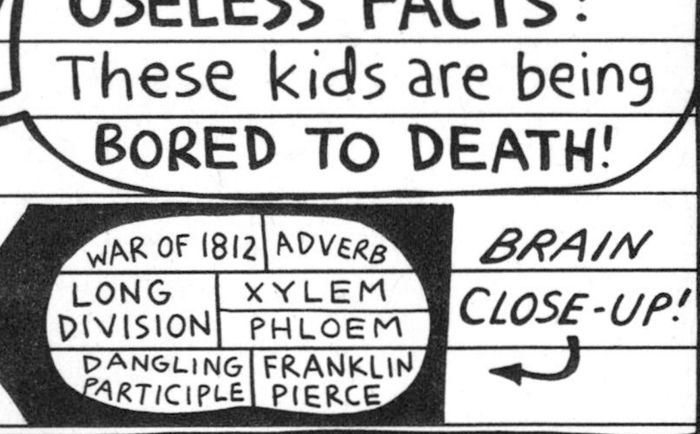

There's only one way to treat this malady!